THE SEARCH FOR THE TEN-WINGED DRAGON

by Jean Karl
Illustrated by Steve Cieslawski

Doubleday ⚓ New York London Toronto Sydney Auckland

ONCE, in a time that both was and was not, there lived a boy named Tobias Cummings. In those days, after three or four years of school, boys were sent out to work. Tobias found his job in the toyshop of A. Butterworth. There he swept floors and cleaned tools and sold toys to those who came to buy. It was an exciting place to be. Tobias thought himself lucky.

The most wonderful thing about the shop, to Tobias, was the fact that toys were not only sold there, they were also made there. And more than anything else, Tobias wanted to be a toymaker.

He wanted to cut a duck out of wood, fit it with wheels, and watch a small boy pull it across the floor. He wanted to fashion a drummer out of tin, wind it up, and hear the soft pat-a-pan of wire drumsticks on a painted drum.

"I can do it," he said to Master Butterworth. "I can make a toy all on my own."

"NO, boy, I'm afraid you can't. At least not until you learn about tin snips and solder and saws and something about dreams," said A. Butterworth.

Tobias puzzled over that. And though, along with sweeping and selling, he learned about tin snips and solder and saws and all the tools in the shop, he couldn't quite understand about the dreams. After all, toys came from wood and tin and the work of strong hands. What had dreams to do with that?

"Surely I am ready now," he said one day. "I know I can make a toy all by myself." He was pounding the final nail straight into a little wooden cart as A. Butterworth watched.

"No, not yet," Master Butterworth said. "The most important learning still lies ahead. My boy, you can never make a toy all on your own until you've found a ten-winged dragon."

"A—A dragon?" Tobias was almost speechless. "A dragon with ten wings? I've never even seen a dragon with two wings. I've never seen a dragon at all! I don't know anything about dragons."

"Be that as it may, a ten-winged dragon is what you need."

Tobias pondered. He thought and he thought. But he could not remember ever having heard of any dragons that were real, and certainly he had never heard of one with ten wings. But to be sure he asked the townsfolk what they knew about dragons. They only laughed.

"No such things, boy," they all said.

Tobias did not know what to do. He wanted to make toys, not just sell them. But how could he find a ten-winged dragon if dragons did not exist?

As days and weeks passed, Tobias argued, he pleaded, he begged Master Butterworth to let him make a toy alone. But the answer was always the same: "First you must find a ten-winged dragon."

FINALLY Tobias could bear it no more. If Master Butterworth believed there were dragons, then there must be dragons. And if dragons did not exist in his town, then they must exist somewhere else. And if that was the case, he would have to go off to look for them.

So he asked permission to go on a search.

"Well, a journey like that is hardly needed," said A. Butterworth. "But you're a hard worker, Tobias. Take four days if you like. See what you can find. And good luck to you."

Tobias set out the very next morning with a little money, a few extra clothes, and a huge sack of food. He was sure looking for dragons would be hungry work.

That day, as he walked into the countryside, the air was warm and pleasant. All around, birds sang and winds played through the trees. There were sheep in the fields and fish in the streams. Tobias examined them all eagerly. But none of them were dragons. Still, he thought, he was too close to home for dragons to have appeared yet.

EVENTUALLY he came to the next town. There he asked first one person and then another about dragons. But they all laughed; they were just like the people in his own town. Except for the blacksmith.

"Ho, boy," he said. "What nonsense. You ought to be working. Come with me. I'll show you my fire-breathing dragons. I could use a strong boy like you."

Tobias had no desire to be a blacksmith, to make horse-shoes, all alike, at a hot fire. He wanted to be a toymaker. So, afraid that the blacksmith would seize and hold him, he ran away as fast as he could. He was followed out of town by a very large dog, which was not a dragon, and fortunately only wanted to play.

THAT night Tobias slept in a farmer's haystack. And the next day he wandered on. There were horses in the fields and pigs. But no dragons. And when he came to a village, the people there were no more helpful than those he had seen the day before. Tobias began to wonder how far he had to go before dragons appeared.

Since his food supply was getting a little low, he stopped at a bakery to buy some bread. And while the baker was pulling out the loaf and wrapping it, Tobias asked once again about dragons.

"Dragons!" the baker cried. "You're just like those good-for-nothing village boys. Trying to steal my good bread by confusing me with foolishness. Be gone from my shop, you thief."

Tobias hurried out of the shop without the bread. He was no thief, but the village boys did not care about that. They heard the baker's cry and ran after Tobias until he was well out of town.

THE rest of the day went no better. There were no dragons anywhere. And as night came on, he decided he ought at least to sleep in a bed. Haystacks were not comfortable. So he walked toward a farmhouse, hoping to find a place to stay, willing to use a bit of his money to pay for his keep. But he didn't even get to the door. There were geese in the dooryard. They hissed after Tobias. Once more he had to run away as fast as he could. Geese, he decided, were worse than dragons.

Nothing lay beyond but a deep woods. And the food he carried with him was almost gone. He settled himself under a low tree, feeling quite unhappy. Worst of all was the thought that he was no nearer to finding a ten-winged dragon than he had been before he left. Master Butterworth was so sure that ten-winged dragons existed. And he was not one to lie. But where were the dragons? Was it possible, Tobias wondered suddenly, that only a few people could see dragons, and he was not one of them? It was not a cheering thought.

TOBIAS did not sleep well that night and started on his way very early the next morning. Two days were gone. He had only two more, and then he would have to be back at the toyshop. Was it possible that he might not . . . But no! He would find a ten-winged dragon. He had to.

He came at midmorning to a town. The butcher shop there was open, and Tobias bought some sausage, but he did not dare ask the butcher about dragons.

He did, however, ask a man on the street, who looked to Tobias to be quite wise.

"Dragons, boy!" said the man. "What you need to be aware of are not dragons but demons. Demons are the scourge of the world."

When six other people gave him equally unhelpful answers, Tobias decided he did not need to stay long in that town. But where should he go? Who could help him? Where were Master Butterworth's dragons? Would he ever find them?

Just beyond the town, he came upon a farm with a broad meadow. It seemed a good place to settle down, eat his sausage, and decide what to do next. But he had hardly seated himself before he heard a great galloping sound. It came closer and closer. A bull was running straight toward him. And behind the bull came a cowherd.

"Dragon," the cowherd cried. "Back where you belong."

Tobias did not stop to find out where Dragon belonged. He dashed over a low fence and down the road. A well-named bull, he thought as he finally slowed and tried to catch his breath.

Was that, he asked himself then, as close to a dragon as he might ever come? Discouraged and upset, he threw himself down on a grassy mound and cried. It seemed he would never be a toymaker!

Eventually, he cried himself to sleep. And even there he was haunted by his search for dragons. All the people he had met on his journey were in his dreams. They looked like one long dragon, all legs and arms and heads, all chasing after him like the dog and the boys and the geese. And the bull—it had wings and flew after him like a hungry mosquito!

WHEN he awoke, the sun had moved into the afternoon sky and all around it were great white puffy clouds. Tobias lay there looking at them, trying to forget his dreams . . . trying to forget how little time he had left to find his ten-winged dragon . . . wondering what he should do next . . . wishing it were a lion or a bear that Master Butterworth had sent him after. Those he knew about.

"There's a lion now," he told himself. In his mind one of the big, puffy clouds had come to look like a lion. He would have laughed at the idea, but he didn't feel happy enough for that.

Then, slowly, his dream returned to him—all those people chasing him, looking like a dragon. And that bull! It was called Dragon, and in the dream it had had wings. He looked at another cloud and sat up. Was that? Was it? Yes, yes, wasn't that a ten-winged dragon? No, no, it couldn't be. But it was. As real as any dragon could ever be.

Tobias stood up. The cloud was moving. It was changing shape. But even so, it was still a ten-winged dragon!

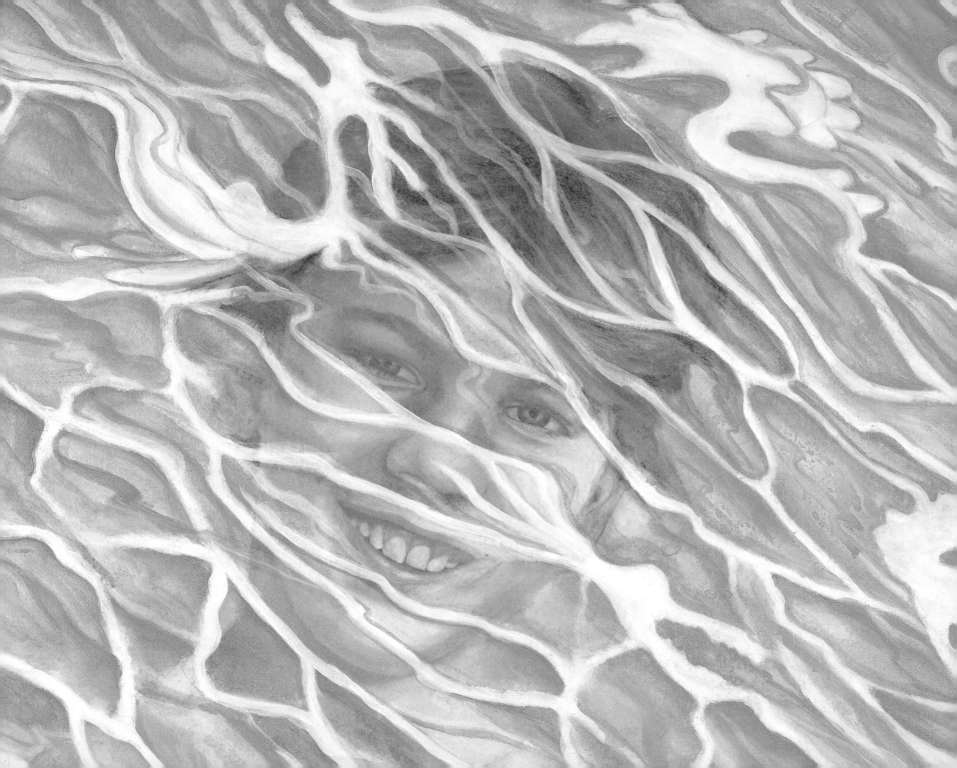

HE looked around. In a nearby field men were harvesting grain. As they worked, throwing grain into a wagon, he saw another dragon: the horses, the cart, the men, the flying grain.

Really laughing now, Tobias started to run along the road. At a bridge he leaned over and looked at the stream below. Ripples in the water made not one but five ten-winged dragons.

Patterns of leaves blowing in the trees were dragons.

A stone by the wayside had a ten-winged dragon patterned on its surface.

TOBIAS felt a great big bubble of dragons fill him from head to toe. He picked up the dragon stone and turned his steps back to the toyshop.

He had come a long way, but the road on his return did not seem tiresome. As he walked and ran and skipped, he kept thinking of the ten-winged dragon he might make with tin snips and solder and a mind that could dream of such things.

BACK at the toyshop, at the end of the fourth day, he told what he had discovered.

"But that's not all," he said. "Give me some tin and some tools, and I'll give you the best ten-winged dragon that's ever been."

"Of course, my boy," said A. Butterworth.

It did not happen all at once. It took as many days as Tobias had traveled away. But there came a moment when he turned a key and a ten-winged dragon flapped its wings. Both Tobias and A. Butterworth watched in wonder.

" A marvel," said Master Butterworth. "Best ten-winged dragon I've ever seen. Master Cummings, why don't you make a tin drummer, one with drumsticks that go pat-a-pan on a painted drum."

"I'll do better than that," said Tobias. "I'll make a whole band, marching in a parade."

AND from that time on, maybe even to this very day, the toyshop of Butterworth and Cummings was known as a very special place. Because there you could learn that dreams can come true. Which was, of course, because both A. Butterworth and T. Cummings knew about dreams and also knew about ten-winged dragons.

Published by Doubleday,
a division of Bantam Doubleday Dell Publishing Group, Inc.
666 Fifth Avenue, New York, New York 10103

Doubleday
and the portrayal of an anchor with a dolphin
are trademarks of Doubleday,
a division of Bantam Doubleday Dell Publishing Group, Inc.

Library of Congress Cataloging-in-Publication Data

Karl, Jean.
The search for the ten-winged dragon / by Jean Karl ; illustrated
by Steve Cieslawski. — 1st ed.
p.   cm.
Summary: A young apprentice toymaker's search for a fantastical
creature leads him on an unusual journey of adventure and self-
discovery.
[1. Apprentices—Fiction.   2. Dragons—Fiction.]   I. Cieslawski,
Steve, ill.   II. Title.
PZ7.K139Se   1990
[E]—dc20   89-34229   CIP   AC
ISBN 0-385-26493-3.
ISBN 0-385-26494-1 (lib. bdg.)

R.L. 2.6